W9-ACS-035

Purchase of this book made possible
through a grant from the
Laura Bush Foundation for
America's Libraries.

THE LAURA BUSH FOUNDATION
FOR AMERICA'S LIBRARIES

Moxy Maxwell Does Not Love STUART LITTLE

Moxy Maxwell Does Not Love STUART LITTLE

By Peggy Gifford
Photographs by Valorie Fisher

schwartz & wade books · new york

This is a work of fiction. Names, characters, places, and incidents either are the product of the author's imagination or are used fictitiously. Any resemblance to actual persons, living or dead, events, or locales is entirely coincidental.

Text copyright © 2007 by Peggy Gifford
Photographs copyright © 2007 by Valorie Fisher

All rights reserved.

Published in the United States by Schwartz & Wade Books, an imprint of Random House Children's Books, a division of Random House, Inc., New York.

Schwartz & Wade Books and colophon are trademarks of Random House, Inc.

www.randomhouse.com/kids

Educators and librarians, for a variety of teaching tools, visit us at www.randomhouse.com/teachers

Library of Congress Cataloging-in-Publication Data

Gifford, Peggy Elizabeth.
   Moxy Maxwell does not love Stuart Little/Peggy Gifford; photographs by Valorie Fisher.—1st ed.
      p. cm.
   Summary: With summer coming to an end, about-to-be-fourth-grader Moxy Maxwell does a hundred different things to avoid reading her assigned summer reading book.
   ISBN: 978-0-375-83915-3 (trade) ISBN: 978-0-375-93915-0 (glb.)
   [1. Books and reading—Fiction. 2. Summer—Fiction. 3. Family life—Fiction. 4. Twins—Fiction. 5. Humorous stories.] I. Fisher, Valorie, ill. II. Title.

PZ7.G3635Mo 2007
[Fic]—dc22   2006016869

The text of this book is set in Whitman and Slappy.
Book design by Rachael Cole

PRINTED IN CHINA

10 9 8 7 6 5 4 3 2

First Edition

This story is for my mother,
Mary Elizabeth Morris Gifford Hearley.
—P.G.

For Theresa
—V.F.

A Note About This Story

Most of this happened in one way or another. But because I am the first to write it down, you will have to accept my version of the astonishing and tragic events that befell Moxy Maxwell last August 23.

chapter 1
In Which Moxy Maxwell Begins to Read STUART LITTLE

Her name was Moxy Maxwell and she was nine and it was August and late August at that. It was so late in August that tonight was to be the "Goodbye to Summer Splash!" show at the pool. Moxy was one of eight petals in the water-ballet part. She and the other seven petals were going to form a human daisy at the deep end while carrying sparklers in their left hands.

Next year Moxy planned to do a rose solo. Moxy Maxwell was just that sort of girl—the sort of girl who even at nine had big plans. In fact, last April when Miss

Cordial asked the class to write a list of Possible Career Paths, Moxy had needed a third piece of paper. Moxy was going places, all right.

She was going to her room. And she was going to stay there until she read every word of *Stuart Little*. Mr. Flamingo, who was going to be Moxy's fourth-grade teacher this fall, had assigned the book for summer reading. They were going to have a quiz on it too—on the very first day of school. And tomorrow was the very first day of school.

Now, Moxy loved to read books. She loved books so much that sometimes she would stay up all night and read. It's just that Moxy liked to read what she wanted to read and not what someone told her to read.

And it wasn't as if Moxy hadn't tried to read *Stuart Little*. She had not been exaggerating (very much at all) when she had explained to her mother earlier today that the reason she hadn't finished reading *Stuart Little* had nothing to do with the fact that she had spent too little time with the book.

"We've been practically like best friends all summer," she said. "Inseparable."

It was true. Moxy had taken *Stuart Little* with her everywhere. If *Stuart Little* wasn't in her backpack, *Stuart Little* was in her lap. When Moxy was in the car on her way to rehearse her daisy routine, *Stuart Little* was beside her or somewhere behind her or nestled under the windshield swelling up with sun.

It was also true that Moxy's mother had found *Stuart Little* on the porch under the broken leg of the wicker coffee table more than once. But that was a discussion for another day.

"In fact, last Monday *Stuart Little* fell in the pool," said Moxy. "That's how close we are."

This is a photograph taken by Moxy's twin brother, Mark. You can see that Stuart Little spent a considerable amount of the summer soaking up sun and water.

chapter 2
In Which We Are Very Briefly Introduced to Moxy's Twin Brother, Mark Maxwell

Except for the fact that they were twins, Mark and Moxy were different in so many ways I could spend all day listing them. For example, Moxy had not yet read *Stuart Little*, while Mark had read *Stuart Little* on the first day of summer vacation. Moxy was always talking about something she planned to do. Mark was always teasing her about something she'd *done*. Moxy had spent her summer at the pool (except Sundays) practicing her part as a petal for the water-ballet show. Mark had spent his summer teaching himself photography. He wasn't very good yet. But he was very much like Moxy in one way—he never gave up once he decided to do something.

wanted to know if she could get another to keep him company. Before she could finish one sentence she had often started another.

"Exactly," Moxy said, agreeing with her mother. "My in-betweens are always interrupted by other things."

Moxy's mother stared at her.

"Remember the time I got settled on the porch swing with *Stuart Little* and a glass of lemonade and a yellow highlighter just in case I read something important, remember that?"

Moxy's mother shook her head. "Refresh my memory," she said.

"You don't remember how Pansy practically kicked the swing with her foot when she asked me to tie her shoe and then the lemonade spilled all over *Stuart Little* and ruined my new yellow highlighter and then Pansy didn't clean it up well enough and a billion ants came the next day?"

Moxy's mother remembered that.

(Pansy was Moxy's four-year-old sister, and instead of reading *Stuart Little* this summer she was learning to tie her shoes.)

Here is a photograph Mark took of Pansy's foot after she asked Moxy to tie her shoe.

And here is a picture of almost a billion ants.

"That's what I mean about being interrupted every time I have an in-between," explained Moxy.

chapter 5
In Which the Word "Consequences" First Appears

If Moxy did not stay in her room and read all of *Stuart Little*, there were going to be "consequences," Moxy's mother made clear before she left to do her errands.

Moxy loved errands. Today her mother was going to the bakery to pick up the great daisy cake for the after-show party tonight. Then she was going to pick up Rosie from the groomer. Rosie was one of the Maxwells' dogs. Mudd was the other. He was part black Lab and part German shepherd and part himself. Rosie was a terrifying terrier mix with long hair that needed to be done often.

Finally, it would be off to the nursery to buy a fabulous new and improved fertilizer for the dahlias, which is the name of the flowers Moxy's mother grew in her famous dahlia garden.

This is a not-very-good photograph of Moxy's mother's dahlia garden. It was taken by Mark Maxwell very early this morning.

chapter 6
Regarding Her Mother's Errands

How Moxy longed to go! It was the perfect sort of errand outing—there was no dry cleaning involved. No stopping at boring places to pick up boring things, like resoled shoes. Waiting for fertilizer would be boring, but—thought Moxy, who was really beginning to think now—I could use the extra time to really dig in and begin *Stuart Little*.

"But Mother, don't you see—it's the perfect in-between. I'll stay in the car with *Stuart Little* while you go in and buy fertilizer."

chapter 7
In Which Moxy's Mother Says No

"No."

chapter 8
In Which
Moxy Considers
Actually Reading
STUART LITTLE

There had been a certain something in the tone of her mother's "no," so even before the car backed down the driveway, Moxy went to her room and moved a few things off her bed and sat down and began to consider the possibility of actually reading *Stuart Little*.

First, of course, she would have to clean her room. A book of this magnitude—144 pages—required a great deal of space.

Just as Moxy was about to roll her sleeves up and get down to business and really dig in, Sam called.

This is a fabulous photograph Mark Maxwell took of Moxy's room after she'd answered her phone and before she'd started cleaning.

"I'm sorry but I can't talk now," said Moxy. "I'm very busy."

"It's Sam. What are you doing?"

Even though Sam was only six and Moxy was already nine, Moxy considered Sam her best friend. That's because Sam did whatever Moxy said: when Moxy wanted to practice being a ballet star, Sam would catch her like *that!* in his arms. When Moxy read aloud from the list of 211 Career Paths she was considering, Sam added suggestions of his own. Moxy had never, for example, considered being a shepherd or writing an advice column for senior citizens. Without Sam she never would have thought of either one.

The truth was, Sam had a little crush on Moxy, though Moxy pretended not to notice and Sam didn't really understand it. All Sam knew was that Moxy always had a plan and when Moxy had a plan something always happened. Like last summer when they had picked up golf balls from the seventh green of the Forest Hills golf course and washed them off and sold them back to golfers for twenty-five cents apiece. It was always interesting to be with Moxy.

"I'm cleaning my room," Moxy explained. "It's a bit messy. Which is the main reason I haven't been able to get around to reading *Stuart Little* yet."

chapter 9
In Which Another Reason Moxy Has Not Yet Read STUART LITTLE Is Uncovered

"Another reason is because I've been trying to train Mudd," Moxy continued. She was speaking to Sam from her new shocking pink cell phone. "Do you think I should call Mom and remind her of that?"

"But training Mudd is number two on your list of stuff you wanted to get done," said Sam. "Reading *Stuart Little* is number one."

"Oh, Sam! If we don't hurry and train Mudd, he will never become a show dog," said Moxy.

"No, he won't," said Sam. Though Sam

wasn't sure of the cutoff date for turning regular dogs into show dogs.

"And you know what that means?" asked Moxy.

Sam couldn't remember.

"It means I will never get to run-walk Mudd around Madison Square Garden in a pair of cute flats on national television. I might just as well cross it off my list of Possible Career Paths."

chapter 10
The Problem with Training Mudd

Though Moxy had not gotten around to actually training Mudd, thinking about training Mudd had consumed a fair amount of her time this summer. One thing she had figured out was that to train Mudd, someone needed to train Rosie first. That's because Mudd did whatever Rosie said. If Rosie barked, "We will now eat pillows," Mudd ate pillows.

The other problem with training Mudd was that Mudd had a serious barking problem. Mudd barked at everything that moved. He barked at a leaf blowing down the street and a butterfly beating its wings and the UPS man delivering packages to Mr. Cloud's house five blocks away. In fact, most of the time he was so busy barking he couldn't hear Moxy when she told him to stop barking.

Just another reason, thought Moxy, that she had reached the end of August without reaching the beginning of *Stuart Little*.

chapter 11
The Part Where the Story Really Starts to Heat Up

This is the part where the story really starts to heat up. The part where it gets a little dicey for Moxy. "Scary" is the word Pansy later used. "Out of control" was the phrase Moxy's stepfather, Ajax, mumbled for some years after. Mark called it "a chain of astonishing events" and left it at that.

Since I am the first to tell this story, you will have to accept my version of what happened next, and I am quite inclined to agree with Moxy when she called this "the Third-Worst Day of My Life."

chapter 12
In Which the Word "Consequences" Reappears

As soon as Sam hung up, he called Moxy back. "I'll come over and watch you read if you want," said Sam. He was always looking for a reason to be around Moxy.

But Moxy wasn't listening. She was looking up the word "consequences" in the dictionary, and it was beginning to make her feel a little ill. It interested Moxy a great deal that a single word—twelve letters that could be erased with a #2 eraser—was powerful enough to make her feel as if she might throw up.

invading army ... conquered. Mexico was once ... Spain.

con·quest (kon′kwest *or* kong′kwest) *noun, plural* **conquests.**

conscience A feeling about what is right and what is wrong. Your conscience tells you to do right and warns when you are doing something wrong. The lie that he told troubled his *conscience.*

con·science (kon′shəns) *noun, plural* **consciences.**

conscientious Showing honesty, thought, and care. Agnes does *conscientious* work at school.

con·sci·en·tious (kon′shē en′shəs) *adjective.*

conscious 1. Knowing or realizing; aware. He was *conscious* of someone tapping his shoulder. 2. Able to see and feel things; awake. He remained *conscious* even though he was hit hard on the head. 3. Done on purpose. She made a *conscious* effort to stop laughing.

con·scious (kon′shəs) *adjective.*

consecutive Following one after another without a break. 1, 2, 3, and 4 are *consecutive* numbers.

con·sec·u·tive (kən sek′yə tiv) *adjective.*

consent To give permission; agree to. Mother would not *consent* to my going camping by myself. *Verb.*
—Permission. My parents had to give their *consent* before I could go on the field trip with my class. *Noun.*

con·sent (kən sent′) *verb,* **consented, consenting;** *noun, plural* **consents.**

consequence 1. Outcome; result. He climbed over the barbed wire fence and as a *consequence* he ripped his pants. She suffered the *consequences* of her bad behavior. 2. Importance. What he thinks is of little *consequence* to me.

con·se·quence (kon′sə kwens′) *noun, plural* **consequences.**

consequently As a result; therefore. The little boy did not wear his boots when it rained, and *consequently* he got his sho...

...ral con-

The army ...

Here is a close close-up picture Mark took of the definition of the word "consequence" from the Random House dictionary.

When Moxy didn't reply, Sam imagined he heard the words "Come right over!" in Moxy's silence and set out for the Maxwells' house.

By the time he reached their front porch, Moxy's room was clean. All the old ice cream bowls and clean and dirty towels, all the magazines and general damp debris that always accumulates over the months of June and July and up through the first twenty-three days of August in the room of a nine-year-old Moxy, had been swept sort of neatly under the bed.

"Take a picture of it, Mark! It may never look this good again," said Moxy to her brother, who was standing in the doorway watching her.

Moxy could be pretty bossy.

"But you can still see the whole mess," he said. "Dirty clothes are practically crawling out from under your bed."

Here is the photograph Mark Maxwell finally took of Moxy's room after she cleaned it. Moxy called it the "after" photograph.

chapter 13
Moxy's
Amazing
Idea

Moxy was just about to get down to the serious business of looking at the pictures in *Stuart Little* when she had an idea so wild, so unlikely, so stupendous, that when she recounted it later, her flabbergasted stepfather said, "And you thought of this all by yourself?"

Moxy's amazing idea was to turn her cell phone off so that she could concentrate on reading *Stuart Little*.

(Let us pause.)

"The sheer genius of it!" Moxy's stepfather later whispered to Moxy's mother.

chapter 14
In Which Moxy Decides Not to Turn Her Cell Phone Off After All

A single word stopped her. That word was "extreme." "Extreme" was a word she had learned from her stepfather. "You have a tendency to go to extremes," he sometimes said when she had a good, if unusual, idea. Like last Wednesday when she had proposed that the family eat only foods that were white, such as bread and rice and milk and some puddings.

Moxy's stepfather's name was A. Jackson Maxwell and he was a famous children's book writer. Moxy and Mark called him

Ajax because "Mr. Maxwell" was too formal and "Jackson" was too long. Pansy called him Dad because Ajax *was* her dad, and Mrs. Maxwell called him Bunny. But that is not part of this story and will sidetrack us and we must move on if we're ever going to get to the darkness now descending on Moxy's horizon.

It turned out that "extreme" was just the sort of word Moxy was looking for as she debated whether to turn her cell phone off so she could concentrate on reading *Stuart Little*. If she didn't turn off her cell phone when she practiced her daisy routine or when she ate supper or when she went to sleep, wouldn't turning off her cell phone to read *Stuart Little* be extremely *extreme* or even more extreme than that?

Moxy was just about to invent a word for "more extreme than extremely extreme" when she remembered the word "consequence," which reminded her that she had to read *Stuart Little*. And at that very instant, just as she was looking about for the book, Mudd began to bark and bark and bark and bark and bark and bark and bark and bark—yet another example of an interrupted in-between!

"No bark! No bark!" Moxy said sharply. But as I've said, you couldn't really stop Mudd from barking. Moxy tried again. "No bark! No bark!"

Mark took this picture of Mudd barking at Sam.

It turned out that Sam was outside swinging on the porch swing.

"Mark!" Moxy called out. "Why don't you try and help once in a while? I can't make Mudd stop barking all by myself!"

"I can't interfere with what the camera sees," said Mark.

"Whatever that means," said Moxy.

"See what I mean about training Mudd before it's too late?" she said as Sam walked in. Then she added, "Why is he barking at you? He's known you for like three years."

"How is *Stuart Little* going?" asked Sam.

"I'm feeling a bit weak after cleaning my room and all," said Moxy. "I think I'd better go have a sandwich or something to get my strength back before I start reading *Stuart Little*."

"It *is* a hundred and forty-four pages," Sam agreed.

chapter 15

In Which Moxy Finds the Note on the Refrigerator

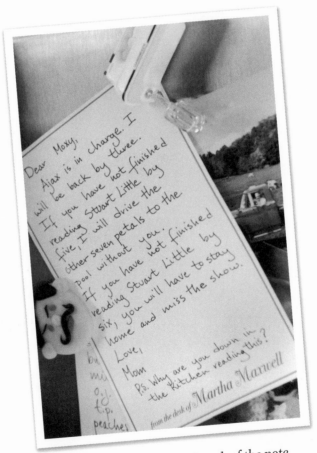

This is the photograph Mark took of the note Moxy found on the refrigerator door when she entered the kitchen.

chapter 16
What Moxy Did Not Do Next

Moxy did not cry. She did think she might throw up. But since she despised throwing up (though she liked the word "despise"), she decided to eat a peach instead.

"May I have one too?" asked Sam. But by then Moxy was already headed for the backyard. Sam took a peach, bit into it, and followed Moxy to the hammock.

"Let me help," he said. He put the peach between his teeth and held the hammock still so Moxy wouldn't have to struggle to get in.

"Thank you, Sam," Moxy said. Then she lay back in the hammock and looked at the sky.

Moxy needed to get organized. She needed a plan. She needed another peach. Another peach would help her think. Once more Sam held the hammock still, and Moxy struggled out. Sam wasn't sure where they were going next. So he just followed her.

Two minutes later Moxy and Sam wandered into the kitchen again. They found Pansy there. She was standing on the counter eating a peach.

Moxy began to pace. This was a clear sign to Pansy and Sam that Moxy was thinking very hard. They'd seen Moxy think before and this was exactly how it looked.

chapter 17
In Which
We Learn
What Moxy
Was Thinking

Moxy was thinking about inventing a hammock that automatically stopped moving when you decided to get out.

She did not even glance at the clock. She did not know that time was running—sprinting is the better word—out. It was thirteen minutes after two o'clock.

Mark calls this photograph "The End of Time: Still Life with Peaches and Moxy's Right Arm."

And then, just as she was about to throw the first peach pit away, it happened.

chapter 18
In Which Moxy Has the Most Brilliant Idea of Her Life

Actually, Moxy's mother disagreed when she found out about it. But at the time, as Moxy said later and many times over, it seemed like a fabulous, stupendous, near-genius idea.

chapter 19
Moxy's Fabulous, Stupendous, Near-Genius Idea

"A peach orchard," said Moxy as she bit into a peach, "is the only thing that will save me." Then she added, taking a fourth peach, "Thank goodness I'm me. Otherwise I wouldn't have come up with this fabulous, stupendous, near-genius idea, and then where would we be?"

Pansy and Sam leaned ever so slightly (you wouldn't have noticed if I hadn't told you) toward her.

The kitchen clock hummed like a mosquito; the *pad, pad* of Ajax's fingers on his laptop upstairs sounded like thunder.

"You're going to have to go out there and plant a peach orchard right now," said Moxy, pointing at the backyard. "And thank you for your help," she added. She knew that saying thank you encouraged people to help you even more.

She handed Sam the peach pit she'd been holding in her hand. "Start with this," she said. "Please." "Please" was also a very helpful word. It encouraged people who might otherwise quit to keep going.

Sam and Pansy stared at Moxy.

"How else are we going to pay for my college education?" she said. It was all so obvious.

Pansy had not blinked since—I don't know—two pages ago, so she did.

"Don't you *get* it?" Moxy was growing the tiniest bit impatient. "When Mother sees that I can make enough money selling peaches from my peach orchard to pay for my entire college education—and possibly dental school too, if that's a Career Path I happen to choose—she'll say to Ajax, 'That Moxy is so smart, why on earth does she need to read a book about a mouse!'"

Moxy was not convinced that Sam and Pansy were using their quiet time constructively. "We haven't got time to stand around staring at nothing!" Moxy exclaimed. "The whole orchard has to be planted and watered before Mother gets home."

chapter 20
In Which Moxy Snaps into Action

Moxy went back to the hammock and lay down. She was exhausted. She'd been on an emotional roller coaster for most of the day.

Granted, there were a few problems with the Peach Orchard Plan. For example, it might take as long as three months for the peach pits to grow into peach trees. But all in all, it was a good idea. Moxy sent Pansy to the garage to get the shovel.

It was a perfect day. There was a light September breeze, but the sun was an

August sun, a warm sun. It occurred to Moxy that she should start reading *Stuart Little* just in case her mother did not immediately grasp the magnitude of the Peach Orchard Plan.

Moxy was ever so slightly annoyed when Pansy started digging underneath the hammock. "Over there," said Moxy. "There's plenty of room for a peach orchard over there." She pointed to a sunny stretch of lawn a few feet from her mother's prize garden. Its location would please her brother, Mark, because he would no longer have to mow that part.

Moxy settled back and considered the curious fact that she had preferred cleaning her room to reading a book. It was peculiar because Moxy hated cleaning her room. She hated cleaning her room so much that cleaning her room was number two on her List of Things She Hated to Do.

chapter 21
In Which
Moxie Solves
the Problem of
World Hunger

Could this be the solution to world hunger? Moxy wondered. Everyone must have something they *had* to do that they hated so much they would do almost anything but that thing. Mark would probably milk cows in Africa for starving children if it meant he didn't have to mow the lawn. She knew her mother would give up all her worldly possessions, fly to China, and pick rice for poor people if it meant she didn't have to keep telling Moxy to read *Stuart Little*. The possibilities went on and on.

Moxy was just turning her attention to the problem of global warming when it occurred to her that someone had better remember to water the new peach orchard. It wasn't hot out, exactly, but it wasn't September either.

"Sam," Moxy called out. Sam was helping Pansy dig holes. "After you've buried all the peach pits, we must, must, *must* remember to water them. Thank you so much."

Even now Moxy's mother was on her way home with the great daisy cake.

Around the time she was thinking about Mark and cows, Moxy had begun to feel a little, well, nervous. She didn't know why exactly. It had something to do with something she had thought about while she was thinking about something else, but she couldn't think what it was. There was no point in thinking about it, of course. It was

.

like trying to remember a dream—the harder you thought, the further away it got.

Even now Moxy's mother was getting closer to home with the great daisy cake.

Suddenly Moxy realized she was in the middle of an in-between! It was the perfect time to read *Stuart Little*! Then she noticed the green hose resting between a pair of dahlias in her mother's prize garden. Again she called out to Sam.

"Sam, when you have a spare minute would you mind coming over here?"

Sam always had a spare minute for Moxy. He jogged right over.

"See how the hose in Mother's dahlia garden is too short to reach all the way back to the orchard? What we need is a second hose to connect to the first hose so we can get it out of Mother's dahlia garden and back to the new peach orchard ASAP—don't you agree?"

chapter 22
In Which Impending Doom Comes in the Front Door

On his way to get the second hose so that he could attach it to the first hose so that it would reach beyond Mrs. Maxwell's prizewinning dahlia garden and all the way to Moxy's new peach orchard, Sam stopped in the kitchen to eat three peaches.

"I've already had five," said Pansy. She was standing on the counter eating what must have been her sixth peach.

Pansy was just about to reach for her seventh peach when her mother walked in.

Reader, I tremble still when I think of the moment Moxy's mother walked into that kitchen at exactly 2:42 on that fateful afternoon of August 23.

"Hello, Sam," Moxy's mother said.

"Hello, Mrs. Maxwell," said Sam.

"Hello, Pansy," said Mother.

"Hi, Mom," said Pansy.

Sam, who was always polite, took the great daisy cake in the big white cake box from Mrs. Maxwell's arms and set it on the counter.

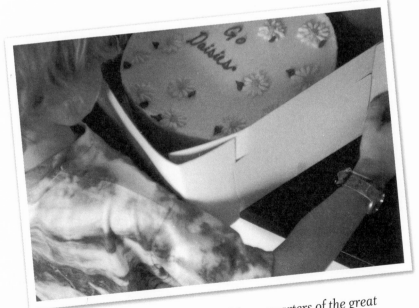

Here is the photograph Mark took of three-quarters of the great daisy cake.

"Sam, would you be kind enough to take Rosie outside and get my dahlia fertilizer from the car . . ." is as far as Mrs. Maxwell's sentence got before it stopped.

"Is that Moxy out there swinging in the hammock?" she asked.

Sam paused.

Pansy paused.

The *pad, pad* of Ajax typing on his laptop upstairs turned back to thunder.

"I believe that *is* Moxy swinging in the hammock, Mrs. Maxwell," Sam said.

"Oh," said Mrs. Maxwell, "was there a fire in her room?"

"Not that I know of, Mrs. Maxwell," said Sam.

chapter 23
In Which Moxy's Mother Slams the Door Behind Her, Which Is Very Unlike Her

When Moxy's mother went out to work in her prize dahlia garden, she was always very careful not to slam the screen door. Everyone else in the family, including Ajax, who was a grown-up, let it slam behind them. But Moxy's mother always turned back around and closed it quietly. This time she let it slam.

chapter 24
In Which Moxy Realizes Her Mother Is Home

Moxy had been frightened before. The first time she and the seven petals had linked arms and dived off the diving board to practice their Daisy Dive, Moxy had been petrified.

But when she heard her mother slam the screen door, she thought, *This must be what "terror" feels like.* It reminded her of when she was eight and her mother told her she couldn't keep a (very small) portion of the money she had made selling Girl Scout cookies (ten percent).

Let it never be said that Moxy Maxwell did not think quickly. Even before her mother's sandals came into view, Moxy's right hand was reaching for *Stuart Little*. She groped for him among the peach pits and paper towels and the hammock pillow and a little pink summer blanket I forgot to tell you about that Pansy brought out to Moxy ten pages ago, when Moxy mentioned that the ever so slight pre-September breeze was beginning to chill her knees.

chapter 25
In Which It Dawns on Moxy That STUART LITTLE Is Not with Her

And now, as she thought about it, Moxy realized she had not seen *Stuart Little* all day or the day before or the day before that. She wasn't sure about the day before that. She might have seen it then.

Moxy's mother was so close that she was blocking the sun. Moxy had never seen a full solar eclipse before, but she suspected it might look a little like this. At least Moxy no longer had to squint.

Maybe this is what "shock" feels like, Moxy thought. It was a little like having a heart attack and a little like what it must feel like to be serene. (Moxy loved the word "serene" because it sounded like what it was, which was calm and clearheaded.)

Or maybe she was not in shock or having a heart attack or even serene. Maybe this was the end of the world.

"Was there a fire in your room?" her mother asked.

"A fire in my room?"

Was a fire in her room a good thing? Was a fire better than not reading *Stuart Little*?

"Not that I know of," said Moxy.

She could see her mother clearly now. Her mother's eyes were quite nice, though Moxy had long felt they would benefit from a pair of aquamarine contacts. But as with many of Moxy's suggestions, her mother had not followed up on it.

"I guess you must be taking a little rest after reading *Stuart Little*," her mother said.

Moxy didn't say yes, but she didn't say no.

"Did you cry when Stuart Little died?"

"He dies! Stuart Little dies?" Moxy exclaimed. "I wish you hadn't told me the end."

Moxy's mother leaned in closer. "You haven't even started to read *Stuart Little*, have you?" She held Moxy's chin and studied Moxy's eyes.

Now, Moxy was fond of the truth. But the truth was not as simple as people like her mother made it seem. Often the "yes" or "no" the truth seekers sought really truthfully called for a "but." "But Mother," Moxy did not have time to say, "we do have a new peach orchard, which will pay for my entire college education and dental school too, if that's the Career Path I choose, and I did clean my room."

Things were quite bad for Moxy now. She'd never seen her mother so calm.

"Are you aware that you are swinging in a hammock and eating peaches and petting Rosie?" her mother said.

Moxy hadn't realized she was petting Rosie. Rosie looked very good. The groomer had done an excellent job. She had even put a pink butterfly bow in Rosie's hair.

This is the photograph Mark took of Rosie with her pretty new butterfly bow.

Moxy scanned the horizon as if Stuart Little himself might appear and rescue her. But Stuart Little was not over by the new orchard. He was not sleeping beside the spade and shovel. Stuart Little was nowhere near the hose and Stuart Little was not in the dahlia garden.

Because the dahlia garden was gone.

chapter 26
The Dahlia
Garden Is Gone

"That's odd," said Moxy. She closed her eyes and opened them quickly. She looked up at her mother, who looked down at her. It seemed to Moxy that everything had stopped moving. That the clouds had stalled over the sun. That her mother had not blinked in a long time. She looked back at the garden.

The garden was still gone.

chapter 27
In Which Rosie Growls at the Garden and Mudd Starts Barking

Rosie growled at the garden. Whenever Rosie growled, Mudd barked. And barked. And barked.

Then Mudd ran. And ran. And ran. But this running and barking sequence was not your average "Sam is here to visit" running and barking. This was more serious. Mudd was so loud and so freaked out that if a UPS truck had driven through the house, he wouldn't have stopped.

Something had moved, and from the sound of it, Mudd did not like it one bit. Moxy looked up just in time to see what Mudd saw.

chapter 28
The Last Three Dahlias in Moxy's Mother's Prize Dahlia Garden Get Swallowed Alive

Here is a confusing photograph of Mrs. Maxwell's dahlias being swallowed alive.

chapter 29
The Great Quicksand Scare

It was obvious to Moxy that the dahlias in her mother's garden had been sucked underground by quicksand. Quicksand happened to be number 42 on Moxy's List of 76 Things That Frightened Her Most.

No wonder Mudd had started barking. It was an odd and scary sight.

chapter 30
Mudd's
Madness

Racing full speed to where the dahlias had once been, Mudd slammed and then slid into that muddy garden. Then he began to dig up the sunken, drowning flowers.

chapter 31
What Moxy Had Known All Along But Hadn't Wanted to Think About

That it was all her fault. Moxy didn't know how. But she would soon. First she had to figure out who had turned the hose on, because it was water from the hose, rather than quicksand, she now realized, that must have sunk the dahlias.

Moxy knew the hose had not been turned on by Sam. Sam was still in the garage. And obviously she hadn't done it herself. She had been thinking hard in the hammock most of the afternoon.

Mark! It must have been Mark!

"Did you turn on that hose so you could get a picture of Mother's dahlia garden drowning?" she asked Mark.

Mark shrugged at her as if to say "What? Do you think I'm crazy?" and took another picture.

Pansy! Pansy must have turned on the hose. But how long ago? Moxy knew Mark had been watching. "How many billions and trillions of gallons of water have been pouring into Mom's prize dahlia garden for how long?" she demanded of Mark.

Mark shrugged. Then he said, "For as long as it takes for a bunch of dahlias to drown."

chapter 32
In Which Moxy's Mother Sees a Dahlia Fall from the Sky

Moxy's mother was looking up. Her mouth was open and her eyes were open, but she looked, well, not asleep, but as if she couldn't believe what she was seeing.

And then Moxy saw it too.

chapter 33
In Which Moxy Sees the Dahlias Fly

Mudd was digging up dahlias like mad. Dahlias were flying out behind him. They were so spectacular, those pink and yellow flowers exploding across that sky, that they looked like fireworks in daylight.

"I wonder if Mudd buried a bone in the dahlia garden," Moxy said out loud.

"Ya think?" said Mark. Mark could be so sarcastic—a character trait Moxy did not enjoy. Then he snapped another picture.

Mrs. Maxwell did not appear to be breathing. Mark did not seem to be moving, but his camera kept shooting.

"*Come! Mudd, come!*" Moxy shouted. But Mudd wasn't listening. After all, he had *never* listened, so why should he listen now? Instead, he kept tossing dahlias into the air.

A dahlia splashed on Moxy's head.

"Come, Mudd, come!" Moxy tried to call again, but her lungs were plugged with the fragrance of freshly launched flowers. It was like inhaling the color green, Moxy thought.

By now dozens of dahlias were airborne. Seven dahlias pelted Moxy's arm; an eighth and a ninth lashed her leg. Three landed in her mother's hair. Two dahlias were stuck in Mark's camera strap, and the red head of a third was tangled in his lens cap.

Dirt was flying too. It was a good thick pudding sort of mud. It wobbled in great gobs across the lawn like chocolate Frisbees and when it fell, it stuck like superglue to anything it found. Including Pansy.

Mudd sent another volley of dahlias out of the garden. Up, up, up they went like water in a fountain. Mudd was almost done. He fired a final round of flowers, and the last of Moxy's mother's prize dahlias slammed into the hammock.

Here is a photograph Mark took of Mudd after he was finished making Moxy's mother's prize dahlias fly.

And here is a photograph Mark took of part of Pansy partly covered in mud.

chapter 34
In Which the Screen Door Slams and Dum...da dum-dum...

Moxy heard the screen door slam and suddenly Ajax was standing there.

chapter 35
Mrs. Maxwell's Unfortunate Appearance

Mrs. Maxwell was on her hands and knees picking up green dahlia stems with no dahlias on them. Moxy was the slightest bit worried about her. But when she saw Ajax treading carefully between the mud and the puddles to reach her mother, it was a relief. Thank goodness Mother had someone to help keep her calm. Eventually Moxy would have to go off to one of seventy-three Possible Colleges and she often worried about what her mother would do without her. It was nice to see old Ajax picking up the slack.

Mudd stuck his tail out of the mud hole and backed almost all the way out, then stopped and went back in again. Moxy lay back in the hammock and put her hands behind her head and crossed her legs. She was exhausted.

chapter 36
The Breath of Ajax Is Felt upon Moxy

"Get up," **Ajax** said.

Moxy jumped. Ajax could be very abrupt. She struggled to stop the hammock— wasn't this just the sort of occasion that called for an automatic hammock-stopping machine?— and stumbled to her feet.

"Now help your mother lie down," he said.

"Mark! Pansy!" snapped Moxy. "Get over here this minute and help Mother get in this hammock."

This is where a photograph of Mrs.

Maxwell holding a little bouquet of flower-less stems should be shown. But Mark was actually helping Ajax and Pansy put Mrs. Maxwell into the hammock, so he could not take a picture. If there had been a photograph, you would have seen Moxy in the corner supervising everything.

chapter 37
In Which Moxy Needs a Glass of Water

"Moxy Anne Maxwell!"

Moxy was almost at the screen door.

"Come back here right now!"

Moxy paused to consider.

"I said *now*!"

"But Mother, there's so much mud," Moxy called. "I don't think I can make it back without risking a fall."

Suddenly Sam was standing there. The second hose was wrapped around his shoulders. He looked like a fireman.

"I'll help you," he said, and before Moxy

75

could tell him how much, how very, very much she did not want his help, Sam was leading her across that treacherous terrain between the back door and her mother.

Moxy was trying to think. *Think harder,* she said to herself as she marched. But the harder she thought about thinking harder, the harder it was to think. In fact, she was thinking so hard about thinking harder that she didn't see Mudd until it was too late.

Mudd was running straight for her. There was a dahlia caught in his collar. Mudd was so proud of his dahlia that when he reached Moxy, he gave a good shake, jumped up, and pulled her down beside him, and just as she predicted not five paragraphs ago, Moxy fell into the whole muddy mess. She could scarcely catch her breath.

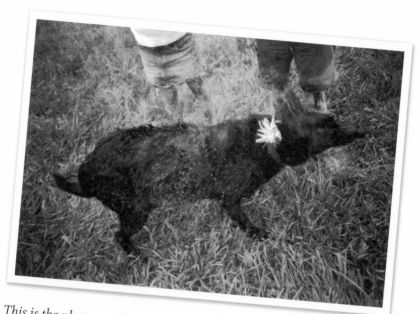

This is the photograph Mark took of Mudd just before he gave Moxy the last prizewinning dahlia.

It was the last straw.

Enough is enough, Moxy Maxwell said to herself.

chapter 38
In Which Mrs. Maxwell Asks How Her Prizewinning Dahlias Happened to Drown

"How did my dahlias happen to drown?" asked Mrs. Maxwell. She sounded very casual. She was swinging in the hammock.

"It all started with the Peach Orchard Plan," said Moxy.

"Peach Orchard Plan?" said Mrs. Maxwell. Moxy's mother often did that—repeated what you'd already said but with a little spin on it.

"The plan I had to grow peaches in the backyard."

"Why would you want to grow peaches in the backyard?"

"Well," said Moxy, "if I make enough money selling peaches—of course, they would have to grow first—to send myself to college and dental school, if that's the Career Path I choose . . ."

Moxy stopped for a moment to look at her mother looking at her. Her mother's face had a curious expression on it, as if what Moxy was about to say next might be the most interesting thing in the world.

"Well," Moxy began again, "if I did all that, I sort of thought you would think I was so smart I wouldn't need to read a book about a mouse. Or anything else, for that matter. Unless of course I wanted to."

The hammock stopped swinging. "You still haven't answered my question—how did my dahlias drown?" said Mrs. Maxwell.

The word "character" was a fifth-grade word, but Moxy had long been drawn to it. As far as she could tell, having character meant telling the truth when it was not absolutely necessary. And even though this struck Moxy as a somewhat unnatural thing to do, she knew it was considered by most adults to be a very good thing indeed, and just now Moxy needed to do a very good thing. Indeed.

"Pansy must have left the hose running in the dahlia garden instead of over there by the peach orchard. But it was my fault," Moxy said. She was so startled to hear herself say this that she lurched a little to the left to get out of the way of herself.

chapter 39
In Which the Age-Old Question "What Do You Have to Say for Yourself, Young Lady?" Is Asked

"What do you have to say for yourself, young lady?"

"It will never happen again," said Moxy.

Mrs. Maxwell felt quite sure this was true. "And . . ."

"And?" asked Moxy. "And I don't blame you at all, Mother."

"What did you say?" said Mrs. Maxwell.

"I mean that in the nicest possible way," said Moxy.

Mrs. Maxwell leaned up on her elbows.

Honestly, Moxy couldn't understand

why her mother would want her to state the perfectly obvious.

"Haven't I been saying for years and years that someone must, must teach Mudd to come? And now . . ." Moxy shrugged. "Well, just look around."

Reader, can I describe the expression on Mrs. Maxwell's face? It traveled from Stunned to Puzzled and back. It moved on from there to places Moxy had never visited before, places like Self-doubt and Despair. It crossed into territories like Hopeless and Surrender, and on the way it passed very near Laughter.

chapter 40
In Which Moxy Forgives Her Mother

"Don't cry, Mother!" Mrs. Maxwell had her head down. She was pinching the bridge of her nose the way she did when her glasses had been on too long. Now was not the moment to suggest the aquamarine contacts. Moxy just knew this.

There was a general silence among the audience.

"What a mess I am!" Moxy said. "Don't you think I'd better pop into the shower, Mother? It's almost time for my daisy routine."

Slowly, slowly, with no help from any-
body, Mrs. Maxwell crawled out of the
hammock and stood up. Mrs. Maxwell was
quite tall. And even though Moxy had re-
cently had a growth spurt, she still had a few
more inches (as she figured it) to go before
she and her mother would see eye to eye.

"I'm going to let you do your daisy routine tonight," said Mrs. Maxwell. "But do
you know why?" It was the sort of question
that wasn't asking for an answer, so Moxy
was silent. "Because if you don't, you will let
the other seven petals down. It wouldn't be
fair to them."

Moxy could not believe her luck.

"But I am *not* going to allow you to go to
the party after the show. And do you know
why?"

Moxy had a feeling she did.

"Because you are going to march home
as soon as it is over and go straight to your

room. And do you know what you're going to do in your room?"

"Read *Stuart Little*?" said Moxy. Her voice was a little weak, though you couldn't call it defeated.

Here is a photograph Mark took of Mrs. Maxwell from Moxy's point of view.

Mrs. Maxwell did not even nod.

"But I might be hungry," said Moxy. "After all that swimming. Do you know how many calories an hour you burn off when . . ." Moxy's voice sort of trailed off.

"You can have a glass of milk when you get back."

"And some of the great daisy cake? Please?"

Mrs. Maxwell shook her head. "And some saltines."

"Graham crackers?" suggested Moxy.

"Graham crackers, and that is it," said Mrs. Maxwell.

Moxy knew enough about her mother to know that this was the best deal she was going to get. So she went upstairs and put on her baby blue petal-covered swimsuit with the matching royal blue swim cap.

chapter 41
The Great
Daisy Routine

I do not have to tell you how spectacularly successful the Great Daisy Routine turned out to be. There were, of course, a few problems. But nothing the average water-ballet fan would notice, unless they happened to be in the business.

It was complicated: all eight petals had to stand on the diving board with their arms linked together until Coach Marjorie turned the Pink Panther song on over the loudspeaker. Then they dived in. Next, *without coming up for a single breath,* they had to swim underwater until their heads met in the middle. Then came the tricky part: they had to count to ten and *at exactly the same time* come to the surface with their legs sticking straight out to form the petal parts of the flower.

Naturally the applause went on and on. It was such a shame that Moxy had to go home.

chapter 42
In Which
Moxy Maxwell
Finally Meets
Stuart Little

The first thing Moxy did after Ajax drove her home was to have two glasses of milk and seven graham crackers. Then she went up to her room and crossed "Win a Gold Medal for Synchronized Swimming in the 2016 Olympics" from her list of 211 Possible Career Paths. Though she had liked the sparklers and the bright blue petal outfits, she had to admit she hadn't been fond of the swimming part.

In fact, as she thought about it, Moxy realized she did not want to spend the next ten years being wet.

Here is a remarkably sharp photograph Mark took of Moxy's baby blue petal-covered swimsuit with her royal blue cap after Moxy had hung them up to dry.

Moxy needed a clear mind and a dry head as she considered which of the now 210 Possible Career Paths she would choose. She thought about adding "Own a Large Peach Orchard Plantation" to her list, but she decided to wait and see how her first peach orchard went.

Then she turned her attention to the cover of *Stuart Little*. He was such a cute mouse. She asked herself why she hadn't noticed that before—after all, they had been together most of the summer. Then she examined the picture of his little sports car. She wondered how he had managed to talk his parents into getting it. Then, as with all the really great stories, Moxy was no longer in her room, she was in the passenger seat beside Stuart Little.

What had she been thinking? *Why ever did I spend the whole summer avoiding a ride in this little car with the fabulous fenders?* was the last thing she said to herself before Stuart Little hit the accelerator and the two sped off.

Here is the final photograph Mark Maxwell took of Moxy Maxwell on August 23. It was taken at one minute before midnight.

ACKNOWLEDGMENTS

Many people contributed to this book. I'd especially like to thank Anne Schwartz, Lee Wade, Valorie Fisher, and Annie Kelley for their seamless collaboration. My deepest gratitude belongs to J. Patrick Lewis and Susan Lewis for their generous help; to muses Kelly Marceau and Scott Marceau; and most importantly, to Jack Fitzpatrick and Chester Gifford. —P.G.

Many thanks to my hardworking, ever-patient, and suitably silly cast of characters: Elinor, Charlie, Aidan, Olive, Anne, Buster, and Dash, and Maisie and Harriet for allowing me to make a complete mess of their bedroom. —V.F.

About the Author

Peggy Gifford's original plan was to become a rich and famous movie star. But after an exhausting tour of Ohio in the role of Winnie-the-Pooh, she decided to become a famous writer instead. (Writers get to spend more time sitting and petting their dogs.) Her MFA is from the Iowa Writers' Workshop. She divides her time between Manhattan and Briarcliffe, South Carolina, where she lives with her husband, Jack; his two children, Erin and Kelly; and Chester-the-Dog. This is her first children's book.

About the Illustrator

Valorie Fisher is the author and illustrator of several books, including *How High Can a Dinosaur Count?*, which received rave reviews. Her first two picture books, *My Big Brother* and *My Big Sister*, were, like *Moxy Maxwell Does Not Love Stuart Little*, illustrated with photographs. Valorie's photographs can be seen in the collections of major museums around the world, including the Brooklyn Museum, London's Victoria and Albert Museum, and the Bibliothèque Nationale in Paris. She lives in Cornwall, Connecticut, with her husband and their two children.